# Frat House Summer

A Heartland State Love Story

Ciree Hawthorn

This is a work of fiction. Names, characters, places and incidents are the product of the author's imagination or are used fictitiously. Any resemblance to actual persons, living or dead, events, or locales is entirely coincidental.

Copyright © 2023 by Ciree Hawthorn



First edition October 2023

**Alpha Reading by:**

*Melissa Smith Proofreading*
(www.melissasmithproofreading.com)

**Beta Reading and Developmental Editing by:**

*EJL Editing* (www.ejlediting.com)

*E&A Editing Services* (www.eaediting.com)

*GCD Editorial* (www.gcdeditorial.wordpress.com)

# Contents

*To all my frat house sisters, you are the real gems:)*

# Chapter 1

## Emma

"You can't possibly be planning to stay in this godforsaken town all summer with all of us away on internships, or going back home—can you?" Taylor whines at me, hanging off the end of the futon nestled in the corner of my tiny, sorority house bedroom.

"Yes, I'm staying here. I have to take that statistics class and there's no other time I can fit it into my class schedule," I snap back, frantically folding laundry into an empty hamper since I ran out of moving boxes thirty minutes ago.

"God. You're gonna be so freaking bored. Where did you manage to find a place for only two months?"

I sigh, "Well, the easy option would be to stay here but because of that stupid, backward ass law about sorority houses being considered brothels if they stay open all year, I can't. It's total bullshit. I'm staying at the Phi Gamma house with the guys this summer. So pumped." I give her a look that says I'm anything but.

"I didn't realize they let girls stay there over the summer! Is that really your scene though?" She rolls onto her stomach and rests her chin on her hands, looking at me quizzically.

"It's the only place I can afford. This stupid class is eating up all of my savings from my job already, so the frat house it is. Apparently they have a designated girls' floor in the summer so it's gonna be me and whoever else is stuck here, shoved in the attic rooms or something."

"Well, at least you get to enjoy some eye candy if you have to take math over the summer. The guys in that house aren't totally unfortunate and they do have that sand volleyball pit out back…" She trails off, twirling her long blonde hair around her finger, and gets a dreamy look on her face, no doubt picturing lots of shirtless men playing volleyball.

"You realize my high school bestie has slept with damn near all the eligible guys in that house?! Eye candy is dangerous under those circumstances."

"Oh, God, I forgot she was obsessed with them! Might be better to steer clear in that case."

"Yeah, well, at least they'll know who I am. I have a pretty good feeling about the fact that she'll be visiting every weekend for the parties or, more accurately—the boys. Nothing quite like trying to lie low all summer with a gorgeous friend visiting constantly, in a house full of guys that are already way too caught up with her." I start to get annoyed just thinking about it and shove things into the hamper even more viciously.

"Do you know any of the other girls that are staying there? Anyone from our house?"

My eyebrows push together as I try to locate a hair tie to pull my unwieldy dirty brown waves back off my face. "As far as I know, nobody from our sorority, but I'm sure there's gotta be at least one or two girls that we'd know. Otherwise, I'll be spending most of my time in my room, reading, working, or just avoiding the chaos to the best of my ability."

# Chapter 2

## David

"How do you have all the luck?" Nick pouts, crossing his arms over his knobby knees and leaning against the wall in the stairwell.

"What do you mean? I got elected into this position. It's not luck. It's just talent. Plain and simple."

"Talent for house managing? Yeah, that's a good one. Let me quickly put that on your résumé," he scoffs.

With a shit-eating grin I say, "I mean, I get to personally welcome all the sorority girls that are staying here this summer, so hate all you want, but I'll be the first friendly face they see."

"Yeah, yeah like I said. All the luck." He turns his baseball hat backward and forward, backward and forward, clearly agitated.

Jake shouts down the stairs, "Hey, are you guys helping move all the spare mattresses to the girls floor or am I just expected to do it all?"

"No, we're coming, we're coming. Not that I am super stoked about being roped into manual labor, but I can't watch you do all the heavy lifting," I tease.

"When are they all supposed to get here, anyway? Did you give them an official move-in date or something?" Nick asks as we jog up the stairs to help Jake.

"I mean, I have a feeling they're just gonna trickle in this week as they get kicked out of their sorority houses? I told them to text me when they head this way so I can meet them and show them the door code and all that."

"Never have I been more grateful for that old ass law that lets us charge them to stay here for the summer while the sororities are closed." Nick puffs, out of breath from one fucking flight of stairs.

"Spoken like a true finance chair." I chuckle.

"Hey, I mean, if it gives the house budget a bit more money for parties this year, I'm all in. Plus, we get to hang out with a bunch of babes all summer. Seems like a win-win to me." He grabs a mattress Jake left in the hall outside our bunk room and indicates I should pick up the other end. "Not to mention the fact will be so far ahead in 'community relations' that by the time Greek Week rolls around in the fall, we will know exactly which houses we wanna be paired with. This could definitely give us a leg up on the competition. Especially if we have girls that hold positions staying here. Shouldn't be too hard to bend their ears after they get to know us." Nick wiggles his eyebrows in what I'm sure he thinks is a seductive way.

"Get to know us, or get to know you, Mr. Master Plan?" I ask, grabbing the mattress and backing down the hallway.

"I mean, we all have something different to offer. I think we could divide and conquer, don't you?"

Jake, carrying two mattresses—one under each arm—and now officially fed up with Nick's bullshit, mutters from behind him, "How about we divide and conquer these mattresses. I have shit to do today."

# Chapter 3

## Emma

Frat House Manager Guy

Sure thing, I can meet you out front in about five minutes?

Drive safe. See you soon!

A tall, smiling, blonde kid comes out the front door right as I pull up. "Hey, are you Emma?"

"Sure am. I assume you're David, the house manager?" I stick out my hand to shake, and he grabs it firmly, pumping once then letting go.

"That's me. Service with a smile. So we have the same door code for all the doors, front, side and back but I will just warn you now that the side door is heavy as hell so just don't be worried if it sticks when it's super humid and feels impossible to get open. The door code won't have been changed, I promise, it's just finicky." He gives me a slightly distressed look, rolling his eyes, as if he's already gone through this with at least three people. Maybe he has.

"Good to know. Do not attempt on an arm day," I joke, trying to lighten the mood.

He perks up a bit at that. "Oh, I didn't realize you lift. Are you gonna be using the house gym while you're here? It's pretty dead over the summer, so you'd probably have it yourself more often than you think."

"We'll see. I don't fancy working out in front of a bunch of gym bros. But if you're right and it's dead all summer then maybe... Speaking of lifting heavy things and putting them down, do you think any of the guys would help me carry some stuff up?" I give my best damsel in distress look and then look back towards my car, well and truly distressed at the thought of carrying that all myself, again.

"Oh yeah, sure. I've got rounds to do but I'll grab some of them to help. I'll show you your room first so you kind of have to lay the land and then you can come back down and grab everything."

"Sounds great, lead the way." I gesture towards the house and fall into step beside him.

He enters the door code, and we go inside. Upon entering, he points to a door off to the left. "This is Mama Jo's apartment. She's our house mom and is here all year round with us. If you need anything or have girl stuff that you need taken care of she's your lady. Other than her, obviously, I will be around, so just grab either of us and we can sort you out with anything you need as you're getting settled. Mama Jo also loves to bake, so if you're in the kitchen, she will find you and start chatting you up, just FYI."

"Oh, I've seen Mama Jo around when our House Mom hosts their get-togethers. She's the cutest. I'll have to go say hi after I've unpacked." I glance around at the surprisingly tasteful decor—must be Mama Jo's influence—before following him up the sweeping wood staircase in the center of the entryway.

"The second floor and the third floor are both guy's floors for the summer so stay out or be sneaky. I have to get you in trouble and fine you if I find you there." He looks uncomfortable at the very thought of having to be Mr. Disciplinarian. "So just, don't run into me, there will be signs on the doors to remind you in case you come home late or intoxicated, but I'm sure the guys would gladly help you to your room if you happen to stumble through late at night." He chuckles and I roll my eyes.

"I'm not too worried about that. My focus for this summer is to take Stat 101 and work my butt off to save some money for next semester. I don't plan on going to the bars or being out late partying."

"Well, you know, if you change your mind or if we end up throwing a party here, just figured I'd give you the rundown."

"Appreciate it," I reply as we continue up the stairs to the fourth floor.

We exit the stairwell and he stops almost immediately in front of a room. "Okay, here we go. This will be the girls' floor for the summer. There's only four of you staying here so you all get your own room and don't have to double up. Lucky you. I put you in the corner room because it has the biggest closet. I heard you were a fashion major and figured you'd come with a ton of clothes." He side-eyes me and I see a grin forming at the corner of his mouth. "By the looks of your car outside it seems like I may have been right."

"Hey, I make no apologies. I like my homework where I can see it and wear it." I cross my arms and wait for him to continue his little tour.

"Our very own Carrie, how lucky for us." He winks.

I huff and enter the ridiculously spacious room, taking in the XL twin mattress on the floor, desk under the window, and the three built-in wardrobes along the wall. I can't believe they gave me this big of a room to myself, "Yeah, I suppose this will do."

"Happy we can meet your already low expectations." He smiles and laughs. "As far as meals go, Mama Jo generally makes a big batch of something at the beginning of the week and has leftovers all week for us but you're kind of on your own other than the mainstays. I don't know if you like to cook or not but if you want more variety, I'll show you the private cabinets where you can keep your own food in the kitchen later. Other than that, the bathroom for this floor is just two doors down across the hall." He points down the hallway in the general direction. "Just the girls that live up here will use that bathroom. We expect you all to keep it clean on your own so if you want to figure out a cleaning schedule or clean as you go, up to you. I don't foresee you all being much of a mess but if it needs to be cleaned, it's on you guys."

"I think we can probably take care of wiping down a few counters and skimming a few drains." I reply, scanning the room for outlets and pre-planning how I want to organize things.

"Okay great. Well, if you need anything else, let me know. The parking lot is around back by the volleyball court and you can park in any spot you want. I would recommend keeping to the farthest row from the court in case there's any stray serves, but up to you. I'll go grab some guys and have them meet you down at your car to help you haul up boxes."

"Thank you, I appreciate it," I murmur, already on to the next task on my mental checklist.

"Don't be a stranger." He waves and walks out.

# Chapter 4

## David

I'm secretly a bit mad I didn't get to help Emma unpack her car. She has that grumpy energy that means she is just begging to be made to laugh, and if there is one thing I'm good at, it's making the tough ones laugh.

I make a note to find her later and introduce myself properly.

After moving two more of the new girls in, I find Emma and Mama Jo in the kitchen making scotcharoos. Those little squares of peanut butter chocolate goodness are my weakness, and Mama Jo knows it.

"Hey ladies. Might I bother you for a little slice of that heaven?" I do my best to mime tipping a hat and sidle up alongside them at the long counter. Suave as ever.

"Oh you, I swear I can't make anything sweet in this house without this one sniffing it out and coming running!" Mama Jo exclaims, laughing at my expense and cutting me an enormous piecc at the same time.

Emma glances over and quickly hides a small smile behind her curtain of thick wavy hair. I feel a little burst of giddiness seeing that. Point one for me.

"Well, if I didn't eat all the goodies you cook up, who would you bake for?" I cry out in mock distress.

"Couldn't possibly be the rest of the house full of men that she's paid to look after..." Emma mutters.

Jo laughs really hard at that and says, "Ah, a girl after my own heart! Don't hold back darling. They need someone to give them shit every once in a while around here. Keeps those inflated male egos in check!"

"I can see when I've been beaten! I'll just take my treat and leave you both to it." I chuckle, heading back out the way I came.

# Chapter 5

## Emma

The next day, I hear a knock on the door as I'm hurriedly unpacking all my clothes to find my work uniform.

"Yes?"

David pops his head in, sees me unpacking and casually lets himself in, sitting down at my desk. Cheeky, this one.

"I don't know what your plans are for the first weekend of summer, but a group of us are going pontooning on the lake and I thought you might want to join? If not, no biggie, but it should be fun. It's just gonna be a small group of us guys and the other girls that are living here will tag along too I imagine."

"Oh, so it's like a house bonding thing?" I tease.

"I mean, it's a select guest list so I wouldn't say house bonding... but maybe chill people bonding?" he shoots right back.

"Wow, honored to have made the cut," I deadpan. He blushes, and I laugh a little. "Yeah, I mean I don't have any firm plans this weekend, so as long as I don't have to pick up a shift, count me in."

"Okay, outstanding, great, it'll be fun. I'll add you to the group chat so we can get carpooling info figured out and all that good stuff."

I nod and keep unpacking my stuff, allowing him to let himself out.

"Okay, does everyone have everything they need? I'm not stopping because somebody forgot fucking sunscreen or a water bottle," David calls out.

I just shrug my tote bag onto my shoulder filled with the veritable crap ton of beach supplies for exactly this situation. You can never be too prepared when a bunch of college students are going literally anywhere without real adult supervision.

About ten of us pile into the two vehicles. The girls group up in one, delegated to the third row seats, of course. I roll my eyes as I squish in between the two other girls that came. This is the last time I ride in the bitch seat, I tell myself as my bare thighs stick to the leather and one of the seatbelt buckles digs into my hip.

Thankfully, the trip to the lake is only about 20 minutes from campus so we aren't subjected to Country Top Hits for very long. I don't know what it is about fraternity boys and country songs but I swear to God it's the only thing they listen to. If I hear "Wagon Wheel" one more time I might actually go insane.

We stumble out of the SUV and head towards the lake where David is already pulling the cover off a pontoon boat moored at the docks. One of the guys is dragging a cooler towards the boat and the girls are giggling back and forth, no doubt calling dibs on whichever guy has caught their eye on the way here.

The crotchety old guy that runs the marina sees us coming and just shakes his head and yells something over to David. David laughs and must reassure him that he's got us under control because the old guy guffaws and walks back to his boathouse, waving his hand in acknowledgment.

As we all pile into the boat and drop our stuff, David gives a little spiel about safety, and where all the lifejackets are kept. Everyone ignores him and just starts digging in the cooler for beers and stripping down to their swimsuits. David looks around, realizes nobody is paying attention to him and trails off, shaking his head and revving the engine. We pull out of the marina and head towards open water, and I settle in with a book in a shady corner under the boat's awning.

We troll around the lake for a while, trying to choose the best spot to drop anchor, and finally settle on a little cove far away from the marina where we will get a bit more privacy—and hopefully not be bothered if we're getting too rowdy.

One guy helps David drop anchor and looks around yelling, "Let the party begin!".

We all raise our drinks in salute and two of the guys set up a beer pong table in the open portion of the pontoon.

The group splits up for teams and luckily we have an uneven number so I can stay cozied up in my corner and continue reading with no one bothering me. It's so nice out of the sun with the breeze off the water. I'm in heaven, just like this.

The games get pretty competitive and everyone is starting to get feisty as the cooler empties and the afternoon wears on. Beer pong becomes flip cup, flip cup becomes boom cup and boom cup becomes a shotgunning contest.

Suddenly, I feel a pair of hands grab me and hoist me off my seat, causing me to drop my book. I immediately start panicking, but try to keep my face neutral. It's that Nick, that gangly kid that hangs with David, the one that thinks of himself as such a ladies' man.

"What do you say we all get wet?!" he shouts with a laugh.

"Put me down. I don't wanna get in the lake," I say firmly.

"Oh, come on, you didn't play beer pong with us. The least you could do is have a little fun after coming all the way out here." He grins and some of the other guys laugh, well and truly drunk now. Still carrying me, he approaches the back of the boat where most everyone else is jumping off into the water and I break out in a cold sweat.

"Please put me down. I'd really rather not get in the water." I wiggle, trying to escape his grasp.

"Oh, come on. It'll be fun! Maybe it will loosen you up a little bit," he teases, and I immediately know I'm not about to win this argument.

I struggle harder to break free of his arms but this kid is surprisingly strong and is not letting go. Suddenly, I feel him crouch, readying himself to jump in and I really feel my heart start racing. Then I'm in the water, sputtering, flailing around and trying to reach for the boat while being pulled further and further away by another pair of arms. On the inside I'm screaming. The second whoever's got a hold of me lets go, I know I won't be able to stay afloat. I look around in panic and lock eyes with David who is still on the boat. He immediately registers my distress and jumps in, grabbing me around the waist and treading water for the both of us.

"What the fuck, man? She told you she didn't want to get in," he yells at his friend as he helps me towards the boat.

I trembling slightly as I try unsuccessfully to push up onto the boat.

David grabs my hips and pushes from below and I'm finally up, sitting on the edge of the boat, coughing up a lung and likely looking like a mad wet cat.

"Just trying to have fun. I don't see why she has to be such a spoilsport," Nick pouts.

I whisper under my breath, to David, "I can't swim. I'm not trying to be a lame ass".

"I figured as much when I saw you panicking, don't worry about it. He's the one that's being an asshole. You clearly told him you didn't want to get in the water." He sighs, "I'm sorry he was such a dick to you. Normally he's not like this, but I think he's trying to show off for that chick over there."

I turn to look and sure enough, they're hanging off the same floaty, making eyes at each other already. Me—totally forgotten.

"Well, thank you for fishing me out. I appreciate it. I probably shouldn't have come to the stupid lake, anyway."

"You should be able to enjoy a nice sunny day on the water without somebody putting you in danger. That's on him."

We head back to the main section of the boat and he grabs a beach towel, wrapping it around my shoulders. I smile up at him in thanks and he grabs my water bottle, handing it to me.

"This lake water tastes like ass, being so stagnant, I figured you might wanna wash your mouth out."

"You read my mind."

On the way back from the lake I make sure to get in the car with David. After the whole almost drowning thing, I didn't really want to hang out with Nick any longer than I have to.

David doesn't mention it the entire ride back and makes sure that I'm included in the conversation, keeping me involved without singling me out. I'm grateful and yet a little confused. I have no idea why he's decided to be so nice to me after I ruined his lake day by being an incompetent mess and making him play lifeguard.

I still don't know what came over me. Thinking that I could go on a boat with a bunch of drunk college kids and somehow not get in the water. *Oh well, hindsight is 20/20 and all that.*

As we pull up to the frat house and people pile out of the car, I catch myself lingering a bit.

"Do you need help unloading and getting things back inside?" I ask David, scuffing my sandal in the gravel of the parking lot.

His face lights up, "Actually, now you mention it, do you mind grabbing some of the soft stuff out of the back? I want to get those beach towels in the wash before they start making my car smell rank."

"Can do." I hoist my tote onto my shoulder, open the hatch and grab all the towels, turning to enter the house when I'm stopped by what feels like a wall of muscle. I look up and David is making very intense eye contact.

"Thanks for helping me—" he starts.

"No. Thank you," I interrupt. "You were the one that helped me today. I'm so embarrassed that you had to fish me out. Normally not being able to swim doesn't come up like this in large groups."

He grabs my chin in one hand tilting my face up towards his, shaking his head. "It's really not that big of a deal. I'm sure plenty of people can't swim. You are just lucky I used to be a swim coach." He grins and my heart melts a little.

"True. Lucky me, my personal lifeguard," I scoff, trying to look down and realizing he still has hold of my chin. I shift nervously, adjusting the load of towels in my arms and he leans in suddenly and kisses me softly on the lips. A towel drops between us. "Oh shit," I murmur, in a state of shock.

"Oh shit is right," he says, looking around distractedly and unloading the rest of the car.

I come around the car towards the house and realize there's a new car in the parking lot that wasn't there before we left.

It's Kate's.

She's sitting on the hood like she's waiting for me and I realize we must have had plans for her to come up and visit me this weekend.

"Oh crap. Did I completely blow you off? How long have you been here?" I asked hurriedly as I hobble towards her with the load of beach towels.

"Actually, not long, only about 15 minutes. Glad to see you were so excited to be expecting me though," she teases.

"To be fair, I didn't have plans to be out today. Things kind of got thrown together last minute." I smile dreamily and look back as gravel crunches and David rounds his car. He ducks his head and walks past us saying nothing and I feel my eyebrows come together in a frown.

"Is he giving you a rough time about living here? I can say something to him, you know," she says.

"What do you mean, is he giving me a rough time?" I blurt.

"Well, what with you being my best friend and all I just figured living with my ex wouldn't be the easiest thing in the world and he'd be a bit of a dick to you."

"When did you date David?" I ask, starting to get a terrible feeling in the pit of my stomach.

"Oh, a few months back we had a thing going for a few weeks. It didn't work out, obviously." She laughs and grabs some towels out of my arms, helping me into the house.

# CHAPTER 6

## EMMA

A few days later I'm walking to class with Olivia, a friend who is living in the frat house next door. Explaining the whole clusterfuck of a situation that I got myself into this weekend.

"How was I supposed to know she's literally slept with the entire house?! I figured I'd at least be safe with someone as straight-laced as David. He's not exactly her usual type."

"So, who is her usual type?" Olivia asks, laughing at my expense.

"Generally... anyone that she can hook up with, have a good time and then not feel bad about not texting when she goes home. I think she enjoys being able to hit it and quit it and then escape back to her regular life with no strings attached. It's one reason she doesn't go here and decided to go to community college back home for the first 2 years. Separation of church and state."

"Well, I have to hand it to her, that's quite the system." Olivia raises her eyebrow and waits for me to continue.

"It's just Kate. No system. She's casual and she likes to keep most things in her life that way and I love her for it. I sometimes wish I could be as carefree as she is. But right now it just feels like a gigantic mess and I don't know how I feel about it." I sigh.

"How does she feel about it?"

"What do you mean?"

"Well, did you ask her how she felt about you and David? After the whole kiss thing." She looks at me expectantly.

"No. Are you kidding me? I was panicking. I wasn't about to tell her I'd just kissed her ex literally twenty feet away from her without realizing it. Not to mention he was super weird after the fact and I got the feeling that he might have seen her before I did. I don't know what that means though... If he doesn't care and is worried she will? Or if he does care and didn't realize we were friends until he saw us talking together. Overall, awkward all around."

"Yeah, maybe, but it seems like you were pretty excited about that kiss before you ran into her. Don't you think that's worth exploring?"

"I don't know how I'm going to explore something that's completely off limits!"

"But is it though?" Olivia gives me a knowing look and I almost trip over a crack in the sidewalk.

"Of course it is! He's her ex. That's against all elements of girl code."

"I mean I would usually agree with you, but it seems like they were pretty casual. I think it's worth asking her how she feels about it and going from there."

"How mortifying. Asking if I can take her sloppy seconds? Kill me now."

# Chapter 7

## Emma

My attempts to avoid David until I can talk to Kate have been well and truly shat on. Over and over again the past week. It started out with him being slightly cautious around me, neither one of us acknowledging the kiss.

Then quickly snowballed into flirty looks while passing each other in the hallways, him opening the door for me as I left for work and he was on his way out somewhere.

Now it has gotten to the point of casual waist or arm touches when we pass each other in the kitchen. Talk about complete and utter torture. I could cut the tension with a knife.

He hasn't brought up Kate, and I haven't brought up Kate, and until I get to chat with her, I don't think I want to. But this whole week I've just felt like I'm doing something wrong even though nothing's really happened. The guys have started making jokes about us too, which isn't helping anything given that it feels like we keep being thrown together continuously during these casual run-ins throughout the house.

I finally give up and hide out in the movie room in the basement hoping to get some alone time without all the expectation that has been building all week. I throw on one of my favorite movies and hunker down for a nice afternoon date with myself.

Right as Satine tries to seduce Christian in the elephant, I hear the door creak open behind me.

"For Christ's sake, can I not get one afternoon alone in this house?" I huff.

"Well maybe you could, but I love this movie, so you're going to have to shove over," a familiar voice sounds in the dark.

"Bullshit. You do not love this movie."

"Wanna bet?" David jests, leaning over and grabbing some of my popcorn. His cocky grin lights up as the screen goes extra bright for a moment. He tosses the handful of popcorn into his mouth, chews quickly and then takes a deep breath.

Right on cue, he bursts out into "Your Song" the same time as Christian, and really goes for it. Building in intensity as the movie does and ending the song in an all-out belt.

I try to hide the shock on my face but fail miserably. I'm impressed by both his vocal skills and the fact that he absolutely and without a doubt knows this movie and this song well.

David wears a shit-eating grin as he takes in my expression and says, "So what do I win?"

"What would be appropriate? I mean, that was pretty impressive," I admit.

"I have a few ideas... give me a second." David gets up and locks the door to the theater room. Internally, I'm screaming and externally I'm trying not to fidget. I'm pretty sure I know what's coming and I don't think it's him insisting that I burst out into song as payback.

As he walks around the side of the couch, he's pulling his shirt off with one arm behind his head in a way that shows off his abs and makes my stomach drop in anticipation. He throws it towards the back of the room as he approaches, kneels, and positions himself between my knees. Holding incredible eye contact the entire time.

"I think I'd like to see if I can get you off before someone comes knocking, but you'll have to be quiet or one of the other guys is bound to hear and get curious. Is that all right?" He slides his hand up to the waistband of my leggings and starts to play with the edge. Just the tickling sensation has me over stimulated and I know this teasing won't last long with how turned on I'm feeling already.

"That seems like more of a prize for me than for you," I whisper, squirming in my seat as his other hand brushes up my side under my loose t-shirt.

"Trust me, it's a reward for me too," he says as he pulls my t-shirt off and grabs me behind the knees, yanking me forward until my back is flat on the lower couch cushion. He then makes quick work of my leggings and I'm down to my bra and thong.

He sits back on his feet and leans in with his face gently brushing at the crotch of my panties with his nose and mouth. I can feel his hot breath through the thin lace.

He gently licks at my clit through the fabric and my back arches off the cushion in response. "Like that, do you?" he murmurs.

I just groan in acknowledgment.

He continues on like that in a slow torturous pattern until I'm gasping for him to do something, anything, to get me off.

He gently bites the wet lace and pulls, sliding my thong down my thighs with his teeth and letting it pool at my feet. My body is humming in anticipation and all the sensations feel heightened now that the cool air is drifting over my swollen flesh. I jump as his tongue makes contact, and the sensation is no longer rough with friction but gloriously smooth. He licks at the swollen bud of my clit, picking up the pace and holding my hips firm with his powerful hands.

A hot wave crashes over my body and I can't stand the feeling of my bra anymore. I reach my arms behind my back to rip it off and fling it across the room.

"Why do you have to go and distract me like that right as we were getting to the good part?" David whispers from between my thighs, gazing up at my heaving breasts.

I hear a zipper slide, and suddenly his mouth is gone as he drags his jeans off.

"I don't remember telling you to stop." I hiss, frustrated and on the edge.

"I can't stay away for long. Don't worry," he says, going back down to his knees. Because of his height and the low seat of the couch this puts him in the perfect position to start teasing me with the head of his cock instead of his tongue and I let out a satisfied sigh.

He kisses his way up my stomach to my chest, sucking a nipple into his mouth and biting on it gently before breaking away with a pop.

"I got tested after my last partner but I can grab a condom if you'd feel more comfortable with that," he whispers, tonguing my other nipple before blowing on it gently and causing them both to go erect at the cooling sensation.

"What a responsible gentleman, I think I like you even more now," I sigh before shaking my head. "No need though, I also got tested recently and I'm on the pill, we're good."

"Thank fuck!" he moans as he drags the head of his dick through my thoroughly wet cunt and back to my clit, making sure the entirety of me is good and lubed up.

I shift my hips, making my needs known in no uncertain terms and he grins. Bowing down again, this time to leave a trail of kisses up the column of my throat before sucking my earlobe into his mouth and thrusting inside me in one fell swoop. I grunt in a very unsexy manner and he lets out a groan as he seats himself fully before pulling back and thrusting in again with that steady rhythm.

His breath catches for a moment and I practically yell, "Not yet!", grabbing his face with my hands and forcing him to look me in the eyes. "Don't you dare come yet."

His eyes roll back and he slows his pace, reaching down between us and finding my clit with the pad of his thumb, applying steady pressure as he thrusts. I feel my lower body tense as the stimulation is heightened and I rock myself against him, harder and harder, chasing my release.

It overcomes me like a sunburst, starting in my pelvis and radiating through my body in pulses. David stalls in his pattern and I feel his breath escape in a rush over my neck as he comes too, shortly after me.

We stay like this, panting and shaking in the aftermath, neither one of us choosing to speak when a knock sounds at the door.

"Hey, the baseball game is on in 15, are you about done with your girly musical shit Emma?" Jake calls, "we want to watch it on the big screen if it's not too much trouble."

I roll my eyes and ask David, "Is there not a sign-up sheet or something? What if I wanted to finish watching this?!"

"No luck with that I'm afraid," he says in a hushed tone. "Still a frat house with very few rules."

"Ugh, figures," I whisper back before yelling towards the door, "give me two minutes for this scene to finish and then the room's all yours, you big bully."

"You're a doll, Emma, babe!" he yells back before I hear his footsteps retreating down the cement hallway, no doubt to fetch his game time snacks and the rest of the guys.

"Now's your chance for a great escape," I tell David, hurriedly tracking down my clothes from where they are strewn across the room.

"Maybe I don't mind them catching me in here with you," he challenges with another one of his cocky grins.

"Oh, stuff it. I'm not starting that whole fuss with all of them right now. Get going and pretend like this never happened." I shove my foot into my leggings thinking about how I—really—need to talk to Kate and hop around trying to pull them on one-handed before he steadies me with a hand on my back.

“Fine, but just for now. We can't hide from them forever, you know.”

“I know, I know.”

Kater Tot

Of course, when do I not need a
break from living at home?

Why does this feel sus?

# Chapter 8

## David

After the movie room incident I've been trying to keep my distance. Keyword trying.

Living with Emma and keeping my distance, not giving away whatever this is, and not smiling like a lunatic every time I see her is much harder than I bargained for. It doesn't help that every time I see her she flounces right on by as if she's not affected by my presence at all. Meanwhile, I have to go take a time out in the house's walk-in fridge so I don't internally combust.

I keep trying to get her alone but there is always some reason she has to run or a bystander that she can pull into the conversation before I have time to broach the topic of us. She's not outwardly avoiding me, she's just avoiding being alone with me. Confusing as hell.

I decide that the next time I see her I'm going to invite her to the sand volleyball tournament that we're holding this afternoon. She has no good reason to say no to that since it'll be a group thing but it'll give me a reason to spend more time with her. And maybe show off my sand volleyball skills, which can't hurt.

As I'm making the rounds of the house getting the count for the tournament, the opportunity presents itself as she walks in from class.

"Emma, we're hosting a big sand volleyball tournament this afternoon and evening if you want to join the rest of the guys in cheering on the players?"

"Who's playing?" she asks, shifting her book bag from one shoulder to the other.

"Most of the house is playing at some point or another but we always try to make sure there's a good turnout of fans since it's a home game, being on our turf and all."

"Fair enough, I guess I can see if Olivia and Kate want to join."

I tense up. "I didn't realize you had a friend coming to visit."

"Do I need to get permission to have an overnight guest House Manager?" she says, her voice a bit clipped.

"No. No. Of course not. Sorry for being weird." I try to internally shrug off the awkwardness. *Don't overthink this, David.*

"It's only weird if you make it weird," she says, turning on her heel and heading upstairs to her room. "Actually, I'm making a unilateral decision, the girls and I will be there this afternoon, count us in."

I am a raging idiot. I don't know why I froze up when she mentioned Kate was visiting. Obviously, I've known they were friends since the last time she showed up. It caught me so off guard that time though that I didn't handle it very well and now I've gone and handled it poorly again.

It's not that Kate and I were very serious. It's more the fact that I know Emma's likely uncomfortable with our history and I don't want it to affect us. Emma is more than just a weekend fling. Emma is the complete package.

My time with Kate was casual from both sides. We knew what we were getting into and we knew what we were doing when we got out of it. I just hope she has said as much to Emma if they've talked about it at all.

# CHAPTER 9

## EMMA

I text an S.O.S. to Olivia telling her I need her this afternoon at the volleyball tournament for emotional support in case it goes sideways. She immediately texts back.

Olivia

Be there in five, fill me in then.

As soon as she arrives I fess up about the movie room sex, that I haven't talked to Kate yet about David, and the incredible knot that I have tied myself in with this whole situation. She listens without interrupting and just lets the moment breathe once I've finished.

"My advice from before still stands. I think you just need to be honest with Kate and let her know and see what she says. Who knows, she might surprise you."

"Ugh, I hate this. I just want things to be simple."

"Well they might be, it just depends on how fussed she is to see her best friend happy with someone she may -or may not- have cared about."

"You make it sound so easy." I catch myself whining and start picking my cuticles.

"Yes, well, it takes a lot of life experience to be giving out this sage advice," she laughs.

Kate shows up later than expected and we turn up to the tournament after it's already in full swing. The guys are rocking fresh sunburns and sand is flying so we quickly find a spot in the shade near the rest of the housemates that are on the bench and settle in for a long afternoon.

"What's the score?" I ask the nearest onlooker.

"Skins are up by two," he replies.

"Of course they are," I mutter, taking in the teams and the veritable feast of man candy on display.

The guys from the Phi Gamma house are playing skins, likely since they have home court advantage, and the neighboring house is playing shirts. And sweating through them by the looks of it. Poor bastards, it's hot as shit out.

My eye is immediately drawn to David as he dives for the ball, his muscular back on full display. He makes the save by a hair and the team goes wild. I cheer with the rest of them and settle in for a good game.

After a while Kate nudges me with her knee, "You know, you don't have to pretend like you aren't staring at him."

My eyes fly wide, and I look at her.

"It's clear you two have something, if you're holding out for my sake please don't. He was way too nice a guy for me anyway," she laughs. "Honestly, I can't believe I didn't think about setting you guys up earlier!"

Olivia shoves me from my other side, "I fucking told you!" she whispers loudly and we all share an awkward giggle.

At just that moment David looks up into the stands, no doubt having heard us laughing and I give him a huge smile. He blows me a kiss and my heart gives a little flutter of excitement. Game on.

# EPILOGUE

## DAVID

The rest of the summer ended up being my favorite. Getting to spend it with Emma in our cozy little bubble while the whole town was away was amazing. With most people gone for the summer it was like a ghost town and we got to explore all of our favorite places without having to fight all the Heartland State students that are usually here during the school year.

She took me to her favorite restaurant on the north side of town that's famous for their baked mac and cheese and I swear I had a near holy experience.

In return I took her to my favorite study spot, a coffee shop that's open 24 hours a day and yet it is still off most people's radar even though their croissants are unmatched. I have a feeling we will be there a lot this fall now that classes have started. Since I'm going into senior year and she's starting her junior year, we will be kept busy studying and applying for jobs and I expect a lot of late nights.

Moving Emma back into her sorority house was bittersweet in some ways. I'm going to miss seeing her randomly throughout the day but it's kind of nice having the opportunity to "get ready" for dates now.

I still just feel so goddamn lucky that she took a chance on me and that I get to call this adorable black cat of a woman my girlfriend now.

We ended up getting lucky in some respects as far as the house goes. Emma was elected to Greek Week co-chair—basically by default—this fall and I maneuvered my way into being elected co-chair for our house. Now our pairing is a shoo-in to place since our friends are already tight and have been planning for the last month in anticipation. Being that it's my last year at school, the idea of going out with a bang with all my guys and my girlfriend by finally placing in the weeklong greekland tournament feels pretty epic.

Honestly, I'm just excited for the egg joust competition where she will sit on my shoulders while trying to smash an egg tied to somebody's forehead before their partner smashes the egg tied to mine.

Anything to get between her legs.

# Author's Note

Oh, my dears! This was such a fun book to write! I think that spicy scene may be my favorite one I've written yet!

The next story from Heartland State will be a bit different...We will be following Mama Jo's sweet, later in life romance in *Love, Lectures & Lava Cake*! I hope you are as excited as I am for this fiesty frat house mama to find her Prince Charming:)

For all the writing updates and launch date news, make sure you're on on my newsletter list (sign up at the link below) or follow me on socials @cireehawthorn and I'll let you know when to expect the cuteness!
https://bio.site/cireehawthorn

# About the Author

Ciree Hawthorn is a voracious reader turned indie author. After swimming laps in the creative job pool—working in fashion design, being a small business owner, and trying her hand at illustration—she thinks writing is the calling that suits her best. Born and raised in the Midwest, she now lives in the Pacific Northwest with her husband, new baby(!) and their two dogs, Arya and Ripley. The whole crew is usually found cuddled up on the couch watching sci-fi movies or out playing pub trivia.